MICHELLE OBAMA

Sarah Machajewski

PowerKiDS
press

New York

Published in 2017 by The Rosen Publishing Group, Inc.
29 East 21st Street, New York, NY 10010

First Edition

Editor: Katie Kawa
Book Design: Reann Nye

Library of Congress Cataloging-in-Publication Data

Machajewski, Sarah, author.
 Michelle Obama / Sarah Machajewski.
    pages cm. — (Superwomen role models)
 Includes index.
 ISBN 978-1-5081-4831-9 (pbk.)
 ISBN 978-1-5081-4777-0 (6 pack)
 ISBN 978-1-5081-4812-8 (library binding)
 1. Obama, Michelle, 1964—Juvenile literature. 2. Presidents' spouses—United States—Biography—Juvenile literature. 3. African American women lawyers—Illinois—Chicago—Biography—Juvenile literature. 4. African American women—Biography—Juvenile literature. I. Title.
 E909.O24M33 2016
 973.932092—dc23
 [B]
                            2015029599

Manufactured in the United States of America

CPSIA Compliance Information: Batch #BS16PK: For Further Information contact Rosen Publishing, New York, New York at 1-800-237-9932

CONTENTS

"I LIKED BEING SMART"

In April 2009, Michelle Obama visited a school in England. Speaking to a group of young women about her own education, she said, "I never cut class. I loved getting As. I liked being smart. I liked being on time. I thought being smart is cooler than anything in the world.... You, too, with these values can control your own **destiny**." This determined attitude has followed Michelle from her time as a student in Chicago, Illinois, all the way to her role as the First Lady of the United States.

Michelle has been in the public eye since 2007, when her husband, Barack Obama, announced he was running for president. Since then, she has used her position to draw attention to important causes and issues, becoming one of today's superwomen role models.

Michelle travels to schools around the world to give speeches on the importance of education.

FAMILY FIRST

Before she was Michelle Obama, she was Michelle LaVaughn Robinson. She was born on January 17, 1964, in Chicago. Michelle grew up in the city's South Shore neighborhood. Her father, Fraser, was a pump operator for the Chicago Water Department. Her mother, Marian, was a stay-at-home mom. Michelle also has an older brother, Craig.

Fraser Robinson suffered from **multiple sclerosis**, which is a serious disease. However, he hardly ever missed work; he was determined to support and provide for his family. Michelle has said her parents' example taught her the value of hard work. Despite not having much money, Fraser and Marian Robinson worked hard to give their children a better life by sending them to college. That has stayed with Michelle her whole life.

IN HER WORDS

"Barack and I were both raised by families who didn't have much in the way of money or material possessions but who had given us something far more valuable—their unconditional love, their unflinching sacrifice, and the chance to go places they had never imagined for themselves."

Democratic National Convention speech, delivered in Charlotte, North Carolina, on September 4, 2012

MARIAN ROBINSON

Fraser Robinson died in 1991. Michelle remains close to her mother, who moved into the White House after Barack Obama became president.

A SMART STUDENT

Michelle was a very smart child. She learned to read by the time she was four years old, and she was an excellent student who attended Chicago public schools. She attended what was then called Bryn Mawr Elementary School in Chicago. Michelle did so well in school that she was able to skip second grade. When she was in sixth grade, Michelle was chosen to be part of a program that let advanced students take classes at a nearby community college.

Michelle started high school in 1977. She attended Chicago's first magnet school. Magnet schools are public schools that offer special programs and classes. Michelle's high school focused on preparing students for college. She joined the National Honor Society and was treasurer of the student council.

Michelle succeeded in school at a time when African American students didn't have as many educational opportunities as white students. Her determination in the face of **adversity** opened many doors for her.

9

COLLEGE YEARS

Michelle did so well in high school that she was accepted to Princeton University in 1981. She left Chicago and headed to New Jersey to continue her education at this famous school.

The hard-working spirit Michelle grew up with followed her to Princeton. She studied sociology and African American studies. She also worked part-time with children at an afterschool reading program. The money she earned helped pay part of the cost of attending college. Michelle was also part of a student group called the Organization for Black Unity. Even with all these responsibilities, she graduated with honors in 1985.

Michelle wanted to succeed in college for herself and also for her parents. She wanted to make them proud.

Michelle spent much of her time at Princeton studying sociology. This is the science of human society and social relationships. Studying sociology helped Michelle understand more about the groups of people she would one day be serving.

LIFE AT PRINCETON

Princeton University is one of the top colleges in the United States. It has a reputation for excellence, but when Michelle attended, it also had a reputation for being socially segregated. This meant the small number of black students at Princeton didn't often mix with white students. Michelle wrote her **thesis** on the experience of being black in a mostly white school. Her time at Princeton taught her how to overcome differences while also remaining true to her own identity.

HARVARD LAW SCHOOL

After graduating from Princeton, Michelle decided to continue her education at another famous school—Harvard University. In 1985, she enrolled in Harvard Law School.

While at Harvard, Michelle gained a reputation for being intelligent and determined. She was known as a student who took time to listen to what others said. Michelle was most interested in learning how lawyers could use their skills to help make the world a better place.

Michelle worked at the Harvard Legal Aid Bureau during law school. This organization provided free legal services to people who needed help with government benefits, housing questions, and other matters. This experience greatly impacted Michelle. It allowed her to connect with **underserved** people. More importantly, it began a career of helping others.

PRESIDENT BARACK OBAMA

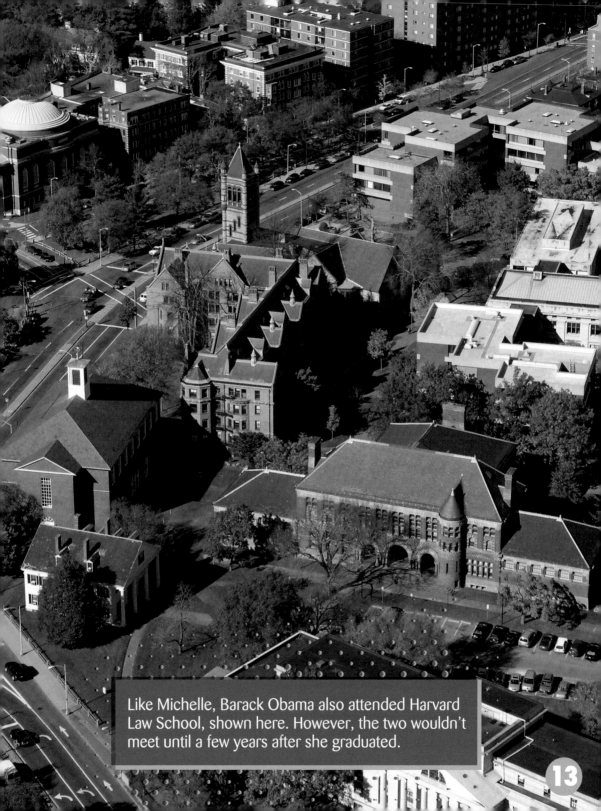

Like Michelle, Barack Obama also attended Harvard Law School, shown here. However, the two wouldn't meet until a few years after she graduated.

SERVING OTHERS

Michelle graduated from Harvard Law School in 1988. She became a lawyer for Sidley & Austin, which is a law firm in Chicago. It was there that she met Barack Obama, who became her husband in 1992.

Eventually, Michelle realized her true calling was to do work that helped improve people's lives. She wanted to give back to her community. Michelle worked for the City of Chicago as the assistant **commissioner** of planning and development. She later became the director of the Chicago chapter of Public Allies, which is a group that prepares young people to take jobs in public service.

IN HER WORDS

"In my own small way, I've tried to give back to this country that's given me so much. That's why I left a job at a law firm for a career in public service, working to empower young people to volunteer in their communities...because I believe that each of us...has something to contribute to the life of this nation."

Democratic National Convention speech, delivered in Denver, Colorado, on August 25, 2008

Michelle's focus on volunteering has defined her life of public service. Her example teaches young people that giving back can help improve the lives of others.

In 1996, Michelle took a job with the University of Chicago. While serving as the associate dean of student services, she created a community service program and helped students get involved with volunteering.

THE CAMPAIGN TRAIL

One could say Michelle's political life began when Barack officially became an Illinois state senator in 1997. He was then elected to the U.S. Senate in 2004. During this time, the Obamas had two daughters, Malia and Sasha. Both parents worked while raising their children. In 2007, Barack announced he was running for president. The Obama family became famous almost overnight, and much of the public's attention turned to Michelle.

Michelle quickly became known as the hardworking partner of this promising presidential candidate. She traveled, made speeches, and met with Americans around the country to gain support for her husband's campaign. However, Michelle still focused on her family first. She's said her most important job is to be a good mother to her daughters.

IN HER WORDS

"According to all the statistics, I was not supposed to go to Princeton and Harvard Law because I didn't come from the right background. I was not supposed to have a successful career in law and non-profit work. And I am certainly not supposed to be standing here today with a good chance of being the next First Lady of the United States. That idea—the idea that I could be part of history and potentially help change the way this country is viewed around the world—is still amazing to me."

Speech to voters in Orangeburg, South Carolina, in 2007

Michelle, pictured here with her family on the 2008 campaign trail, had to quickly adapt to life in the public eye after Barack's popularity with voters began to rise.

THE FIRST LADY

Throughout the 2008 presidential election season, Michelle became known for her great public speaking skills. She gained a reputation for being open, honest, and direct. To the public, Michelle seemed very smart but also naturally likeable. She helped people see Barack that way, too. Many political analysts say these aspects of Michelle's personality helped win voters' support.

In November 2008, Barack Obama was elected president of the United States. He became the first African American president. Michelle became the first African American First Lady of the United States. Just decades ago, the idea of an African American family living in the White House seemed impossible. However, both Barack and Michelle have proven that race doesn't have to be a barrier to success.

IN HER WORDS

"One day...your sons and daughters will tell their own children about what we did together in this election. They'll tell them how this time, we listened to our hopes, instead of our fears. How this time, we decided to stop doubting and to start dreaming. How this time, in this great country...we committed ourselves to building the world as it should be."

Democratic National Convention speech, delivered in Denver, Colorado, on August 25, 2008

Barack and Michelle have proven that anything's possible through hard work and the support of people who believe in you.

BECOMING A ROLE MODEL

Michelle Obama has dedicated herself to many important causes. During her husband's first year as president, she volunteered at homeless shelters and soup kitchens in Washington, D.C. She visited schools to talk about the importance of volunteering. She's also helped raise awareness of the challenges faced by military families. Michelle's hardworking spirit—combined with her efforts to get out in the community and work alongside people—have made her not just a First Lady, but a role model.

As Michelle grew into her role as First Lady, she gained a stronger sense of how she wanted to use her position to help others. After working with schoolchildren to plant a garden on the White House lawn, she was **inspired** to launch a healthy lifestyle program for kids, which is called Let's Move!

Michelle isn't afraid to get her hands dirty! Here, she's pictured planting vegetables with students in the White House Kitchen Garden.

LET'S MOVE!

Let's Move! was launched in 2010 to help fight childhood **obesity** in the United States. The program teaches children and adults how to make healthy lifestyle choices. Michelle's commitment to this cause was clear from the start. At the program's launch, she said, "Let's give our kids what they need to have the future they deserve."

Michelle has used this campaign to change the nutrition information available to kids. She wants to make it easy and affordable for families to make healthy choices. The Let's Move! campaign accomplishes this by providing information about food and exercise on its website: www.letsmove.gov. It's also worked to bring fresh fruits and vegetables to inner-city areas, and it's partnered with major food companies to provide healthier meals in schools.

GET MOVING!

Are you ready to get involved with the Let's Move! campaign? It's easy! One of the first ways to get started is to go to the campaign's website. It has all the information you need to learn how to make healthy diet and exercise choices, including meal plans and exercise tips. You can search for Let's Move! programs and events in your area. There's also information on how your parents and school can get involved.

Michelle leads by example to show how exercising can be fun. She's invited students to the White House to play basketball and participate in other fun, physical activities. She's even appeared on popular television shows to show off her dance moves!

SUPPORTING AMERICA'S HEROES

Countless servicemen and servicewomen have protected and continue to protect the United States. However, the challenges they and their families face are often overlooked. In 2011, Michelle and Dr. Jill Biden launched Joining Forces, which is a group that encourages people and businesses to support active service members, **veterans**, and their families.

The Joining Forces **initiative** works to make sure all people who've served the United States have access to education and jobs, as well as physical and mental health services.

In 2014, Michelle focused on a **unique** group within the military—women. She met with over 200 servicewomen and female veterans to discuss skills needed to adjust to a life and job at home after time overseas.

IN HER WORDS

"You might have your ups and downs, but I want you to know that this whole country believes in you, and we've got your backs. So we're going to keep rallying this country to serve you as well as you've served us."
Speech delivered at the Women Veterans Career Development Forum in November 2014

Dr. Jill Biden is the wife of Barack Obama's vice president, Joe Biden. Both she and Michelle are determined to help those who've served in the U.S. military.

#REACHHIGHER

In 2014, Michelle launched the Reach Higher initiative as part of her continuing mission to encourage young people to value their education. This initiative encourages students to continue their education after high school. The program works with professional training programs, community colleges, and four-year colleges and universities to give students the tools and information they need to take the next step in their education.

In 2015, the First Lady invited all students who had committed to going to college to celebrate something called "Signing Day." On May 1, students around the country wore clothing with their future college's name on it, took pictures, and shared them on the Internet. Adults also got involved by sending messages of support and encouragement to the next generation of college students.

Michelle connects with young people by using their favorite social media platforms, such as Twitter and Instagram. On Signing Day, the First Lady used the **hashtag** #ReachHigher to find and share pictures posted by students. She even personally congratulated them!

LET GIRLS LEARN

Michelle has worked to support educational opportunities in the United States and around the world. She helped launch the Let Girls Learn initiative, which encourages continuing education for young women around the world. It's Michelle's hope that this initiative will give the millions of girls around the world who aren't in school access to education. Michelle has traveled around the world spreading the word about this initiative and the importance of education for young women everywhere.

A TRUE ROLE MODEL

Michelle has been a very active First Lady who truly cares about serving the people of the United States. During her time in the White House, she's helped raise awareness for healthier lifestyle habits, has brought awareness to the challenges faced by people in the military, and has inspired young people to continue their education. She's also supported her husband and raised a family on one of the world's most public stages.

From her early days as a law student working to help underserved people to her time as First Lady, Michelle has become a role model because of her dedication to helping others. It's certain that she'll continue to be a role model long after she leaves the White House.

IN HER WORDS

"Success isn't about how much money you make. It's about the difference you make in people's lives."
Democratic National Convention speech, delivered in Charlotte, North Carolina, on September 4, 2012

Michelle has set a strong example of public service not just for her daughters, but also for young people around the world.

TIMELINE

January 17, 1964: Michelle is born in Chicago, Illinois.

1977: Michelle begins high school at Chicago's first magnet school.

1981: Michelle begins her studies at Princeton University.

1985: Michelle enrolls in Harvard Law School.

1988: Michelle accepts a job with the Chicago law firm Sidley & Austin.

1992: Michelle marries Barack Obama.

1996 : Michelle becomes the associate dean of student services for the University of Chicago.

2008: Barack is elected president of the United States. Michelle becomes the first African American First Lady.

2010 : Michelle launches Let's Move! to fight childhood obesity in the United States.

2011: Michelle launches Joining Forces with Dr. Jill Biden.

2012: Barack wins a second term as president, making Michelle the First Lady for another four years.

2014 : Michelle launches Reach Higher.

GLOSSARY

adversity: Difficulties.

commissioner: An officer in charge of a public service department.

destiny: The events that will happen to a person in the future.

hashtag: A word or phrase written after the pound sign, or hash mark (#), on a social media platform that classifies it to make it easier to search for.

initiative: An act or strategy to improve a situation.

inspire: To move someone to do something great.

multiple sclerosis: A disease that gets worse over time and causes damage to the nerves and spinal cord.

obesity: The condition of being significantly overweight.

thesis: A long essay involving research that is written to earn a college degree.

underserved: Not given access to certain important services, such as health and social services.

unique: Special or different from anything else.

veteran: A person who has served in the military.

INDEX

WEBSITES

Due to the changing nature of Internet links, PowerKids Press has developed an online list of websites related to the subject of this book. This site is updated regularly. Please use this link to access the list: www.powerkidslinks.com/sprwmn/mobama